Note to parents, carers and teachers

Read it yourself is a series of modern stories, favourite characters and traditional tales written in a simple way for children who are learning to read. The books can be read independently or as part of a guided reading session.

Each book is carefully structured to include many high-frequency words vital for first reading. The sentences on each page are supported closely by pictures to help with understanding, and to offer lively details to talk about.

The books are graded into four levels that progressively introduce wider vocabulary and longer stories as a reader's ability and confidence grows.

Ideas for use

- Begin by looking through the book and talking about the pictures. Has your child heard this story before?

- Help your child with any words he does not know, either by helping him to sound them out or supplying them yourself.

- Developing readers can be concentrating so hard on the words that they sometimes don't fully grasp the meaning of what they're reading. Answering the puzzle questions at the end of the book will help with understanding.

For more information and advice on Read it yourself and book banding, visit **www.ladybird.com/readityourself**

Book Band
6

Level 2 is ideal for children who have received some reading instruction and can read short, simple sentences with help.

Special features:

Frequent repetition of main story words and phrases

Short, simple sentences

Once there was a happy princess.

She loved to play by the river with her golden ball.

6

7

Careful match between story and pictures

One day, the golden ball fell into the river.

Just then, up jumped a frog.

"If I get your ball back, will you make me a promise?" he said.

Large, clear type

8

9

Educational Consultant: Geraldine Taylor
Book Banding Consultant: Kate Ruttle

A catalogue record for this book is available from the British Library

Published by Ladybird Books Ltd
80 Strand, London, WC2R 0RL
A Penguin Company

002

ISBN: 978-0-72328-058-3

Printed in China

The Princess
and the Frog

Illustrated by Marta Cabrol

Once there was
a happy princess.

She loved to play by the
river with her golden ball.

One day, the golden ball fell into the river.

Just then, up jumped a frog.

"If I get your ball back, will you make me a promise?" he said.

"I will," the princess promised.

"You must let me sit with you, eat with you and sleep on your bed," said the frog.

"I promise," said the princess.

So the frog jumped into the river and got the golden ball back.

The princess was so happy to have it back.

The next day, the frog
jumped up to the castle.

"Princess, I would like to
sit with you," he said.

"Yuck!" said the princess.

"If you make a promise, you must keep it," said the king.

So the princess let the frog sit with her.

Then the frog said,
"Princess, I would like
to eat with you, too."

"Yuck!" said the princess.

"You must keep your promise," said the king.

So the princess let the frog eat with her.

21

Then the frog said,
"I would like to sleep
on your bed, too."

"Yuck!" said the princess.

"You must keep your promise," said the king.

So the princess let the frog jump up on her bed.

Just then, the frog turned
into a prince!

A spell had turned him
into a frog. The princess
had kept her promise
and broken the spell.

The prince and princess fell in love and they got married.

They kept the golden ball in the castle, too.

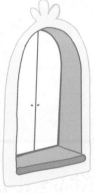

How much do you remember about the story of **The Princess and the Frog**? Answer these questions and find out!

- **What does the princess drop in the river?**

- **Who tells the princess to keep her promise?**

- **Where does the frog want to sleep?** Princess's bed

- **What does the frog turn into?**

Look at the pictures and match them to the story words.

princess

frog

golden ball ①

king ②

prince ④

Read it yourself with Ladybird

Tick the books you've read!

For beginner readers who can read short, simple sentences with help.

Level 2

- Beauty and the Beast ☑
- Chicken Licken ☐
- Rumpelstiltskin ☑
- Sleeping Beauty ☐
- The Gingerbread Man ☐
- Dan's Dragon ☑
- Little Red Riding Hood ☑
- Nature Trail ☑
- Sports Day ☑
- Pirate School ☐
- Sly Fox and Red Hen ☑
- Jemima Puddle-Duck ☐
- The Three Little Pigs ☐
- Why Lion Roarrrs! ☐
- The Big Race ☑
- Town Mouse and Country Mouse ☑
- School Bus Trip ☑
- Topsy and Tim Go to London ☑
- The Princess and the Frog ☑
- Treehouse Rescue ☑

For more confident readers who can read simple stories with help.

Level 3

- YOU won't like this present as much as I DO! ☑
- The Elves and the Shoemaker ☑
- Hansel and Gretel ☐
- Harry and the Bucketful of Dinosaurs ☐
- Jack and the Beanstalk ☐
- The Red Knight ☐
- Fury on Music Island ☐
- Poppet Stows Away ☑
- Rapunzel ☐
- Aladdin ☐
- The Jungle Book ☐
- Roxy and the Great Escape ☐
- Angry Birds Chill Out Chuck! ☑
- Angry Birds Bomb's Best Birthday ☐